S0-BRC-049

WITHDRAWN

No longer the property of the
Boston Public Library.
Sale of this material benefits the Library.

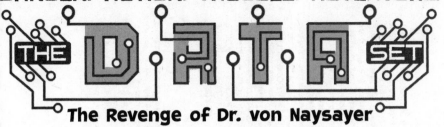

DANGER! ACTION! TROUBLE! ADVENTURE!

THE DATA SET

The Revenge of Dr. von Naysayer

By Ada Hopper
Illustrated by Rafael Kirschner of Glass House Graphics

LITTLE SIMON
New York London Toronto Sydney New Delhi

If you purchased this book without a cover, you should be aware that this book is stolen property. It was reported as "unsold and destroyed" to the publisher, and neither the author nor the publisher has received any payment for this "stripped book."

This book is a work of fiction. Any references to historical events, real people, or real places are used fictitiously. Other names, characters, places, and events are products of the author's imagination, and any resemblance to actual events or places or persons, living or dead, is entirely coincidental.

LITTLE SIMON

An imprint of Simon & Schuster Children's Publishing Division

1230 Avenue of the Americas, New York, New York 10020

First Little Simon paperback edition March 2023

Copyright © 2023 by Simon & Schuster, Inc.

Also available in a Little Simon hardcover edition

All rights reserved, including the right of reproduction in whole or in part in any form.

LITTLE SIMON is a registered trademark of Simon & Schuster, Inc., and associated colophon is a trademark of Simon & Schuster, Inc.

For information about special discounts for bulk purchases, please contact Simon & Schuster Special Sales at 1-866-506-1949 or business@simonandschuster.com.

The Simon & Schuster Speakers Bureau can bring authors to your live event. For more information or to book an event contact the Simon & Schuster Speakers Bureau at 1-866-248-3049 or visit our website at www.simonspeakers.com.

Designed by Joaahn Kwon

Manufactured in the United States of America 0223 LAK

10 9 8 7 6 5 4 3 2 1

This book has been cataloged with the Library of Congress.

ISBN 978-1-6659-1595-3 (hc)

ISBN 978-1-6659-1594-6 (pbk)

ISBN 978-1-6659-1596-0 (ebook)

CONTENTS

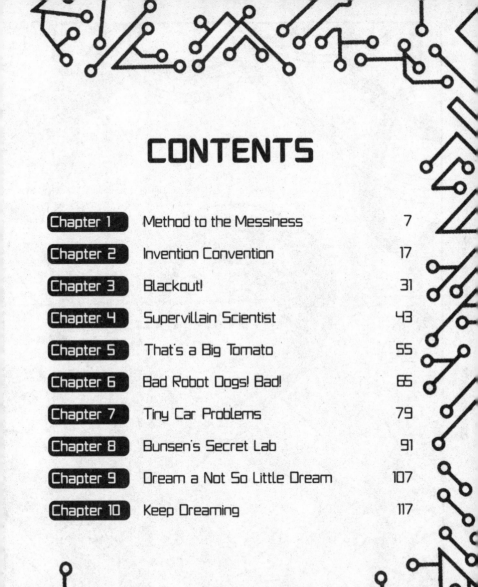

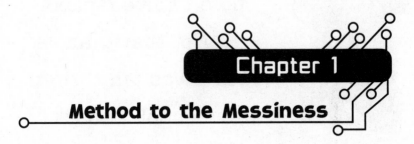

Chapter 1

Method to the Messiness

"Has anyone seen my dinosaur figurine?" Gabe poked his head over a mound of tangled wires in Dr. Bunsen's lab. "I put it on the lab table, but now I can't find it."

"I'll bet it's with my missing granola bar," said Cesar. "My snacks are always missing!"

"That's because you ate it on the way here," Olive replied.

"No, that granola bar was my first after-school snack," Cesar corrected her. "My first after-school snack keeps me from getting grumpy." Cesar's stomach rumbled. "Seriously, where's my granola bar?"

"It's no wonder we can't find anything," Laura said as she stumbled over scattered robot pieces. "This lab is a mess!"

It was true. The lab was a wreck. The four whiz kid friends—known as the DATA Set—were used to their neighbor's wild lab. But things were getting out of control.

"Maybe there's a method to the messiness," Gabe said. "Lots of famous scientists were super messy—Albert Einstein, Thomas Edison."

Laura shook her head. "I could never get anything done if my workshop looked like this."

"Me either," said Olive. "That's what I like most about math. It's neat and orderly."

"What about theoretical math? It can get messy," Gabe pointed out.

Both he and Olive were very good at math, and he liked debating with her sometimes.

"Only because it hasn't been solved yet," Olive said.

"Sometimes creative geniuses need mess in order to make a breakthrough," Gabe countered.

As if on cue, Dr. Bunsen stumbled out with a pile of gizmos.

"Oh, can we help you?" Laura asked.

"No time—no time!" he cried as he dropped the pile with a clatter. "My deadline is tomorrow and there's simply no time!"

"Maybe we should get out of the way," Gabe suggested to his friends.

"Are you leaving?" Dr. Bunsen asked. "I apologize—I'm not quite myself. The big convention is tomorrow. And it's more important than ever that things go right!"

"Do you mean the Invention Convention?" Olive asked eagerly. "Will you be presenting at it?"

"Yes, yes, I certainly shall, " Dr. Bunsen said. "And so shall he. The one who calls me 'too mad and too messy.'"

Before the DATA Set could ask who "he" was, Dr. Bunsen was on to his next thought.

"Oh, you four will come, won't you?" the doctor asked as he produced four VIP tickets.

"You bet!" the kids cried.

They knew tomorrow was a big deal for Dr. Bunsen, and they wouldn't miss it for the world!

Chapter 2

Invention Convention

"The next morning, the four friends rode their bikes to the Newtonburg Convention Center. A large crowd was already gathered.

"Hey, look!" Cesar exclaimed. "It's Dr. Bunsen!"

"Where?" Olive scanned the crowd. "I don't see him."

"Up there!" Cesar pointed.

There were banners hanging around the hall with pictures of the presenting scientists. To the kids' surprise, Dr. Bunsen's face was on the biggest one.

"Wow." Gabe whistled. "Dr. B is kind of a big deal now."

"Remember when we first sold him chocolate bars?" Laura asked. "We didn't even know who he was. Now he's famous!"

The kids checked out the other displays.

"Hey, who's that grumpy scientist on the banner behind him?" Olive pointed to a stern-looking man with pursed lips.

"Don't know." Cesar shrugged. "But I think he could use a snack."

"Are you sure we haven't seen him before?" Laura asked thoughtfully. "He looks kind of familiar."

"Maybe he was on the news," Gabe said with a shrug. "Let's go inside and find out!"

The kids followed the crowd into the massive hall and marveled at all the inventions on display.

"Check it out!" Laura shouted, giddy with excitement. "It's a dartboard with robot darts that hit a bull's-eye every time!"

The kids watched as Laura took aim and hit the bull's-eye perfectly. Then they moved on to a humongous display behind glass.

"No way!" cried Cesar. "It's a robo-beehive that collects honey without ever disturbing the bees!"

Booth by booth, the kids' eyes grew wider. There were underwater treadmills and dogs that were robots. There was even a hologram that, to Gabe and Olive's delight, let you debate mathematical concepts with a simulation of Albert Einstein himself.

After making their rounds, the kids decided it was time to track down Dr. Bunsen.

"Let's find Dr. B's booth," Laura said. "He should be in the VIP section."

The DATA Set rounded the corner to where the popular presenters were stationed—and almost crashed into the grumpy-looking scientist they'd seen on the banner.

The man nearly dropped a glass orb he was carrying.

"Oh, I'm sorry. Excuse us," Gabe apologized. "We're looking for Dr. Bunsen. Do you know where he is?"

The scientist peered down at the children.

"Are you friends with Gustav?"
His voice had a heavy accent. "I
should have known. Carelessness
seems to follow him, no?"

The scientist brushed past them
without another word.

"Man, he really needs a snack,"
Cesar muttered as he watched him
leave.

"Oh my gosh, you guys!" Laura grabbed her friends' arms. "I just remembered where I've seen him before. That's Dr. von Naysayer— Dr. Bunsen's old partner!"

Chapter 3

Blackout!

"His old partner?" Olive asked. "You mean the man we saw in Dr. B's memories? You know, when we traveled through his body in the Bunsen Cold Buster 3000?"

The DATA Set watched as Dr. von Naysayer set his invention before the growing crowd.

Cesar shuddered. "Umm, don't remind me. I still have nightmares about Herm the Germ."

"They have not been partners for years," Laura continued. "But I recognize him from a news program Dr. B had on in his lab one time."

A hush fell over the crowd as Dr. von Naysayer clapped his hands.

"Welcome!" he said with a stiff smile. "I am quite pleased to present the future of science."

Naysayer held up the glass orb he had almost dropped earlier. It was now pulsating with glowing energy.

"After many years of careful work," Naysayer continued, "I have developed the most powerful form of portable energy possible: a plasma battery. Behold!"

Naysayer placed the orb on its activation base, and little flashes of lightning with nerve-like endings stretched out from the center. The crowd *ooohed* and *ahhhed* until . . .

FLASH!

All the lights in the giant room suddenly went out. Everything was plunged into darkness.

"What's going on?" Olive called in alarm.

"It's clearly the end of the world!" cried Cesar as he leaped into Gabe's arms.

"Oof!" Gabe huffed as he held his friend. "It's not the end of the world, Cesar. So quit acting like a baby or I'm going to burp you."

"I'm not acting like a baby . . . *you* are acting like a baby," whispered Cesar as he pulled his thumb out of his mouth.

"Relax, everyone," said Laura. "Naysayer's invention must have blown a fuse."

"Phew," said Cesar. "For a moment there, I thought Naysayer might be a supervillain and this was his evil plan."

"What evil plan?" said Olive. "Turning out the lights?"

The others giggled, but Cesar didn't laugh.

"No, like, what if that orb invention sucked up all the energy?" he said. "And now he's going to use all that energy to trap us?"

"Us?" asked Gabe. "Why would he trap us?"

"Um, do supervillains need reasons?!" snapped Cesar. "No! They are just, like, super bad!"

A small spark flickered above the DATA Set, followed by another and another.

"See, the lights are coming back on," said Olive. "It's fine."

Then the ground started to shake and rumble. The small sparks from above grew into full bolts of electricity that bounced around the room.

"Okay, maybe Cesar was right," said Laura. "I think it's time to run!"

Laura darted forward but smacked into something hard and invisible.

"Is it some kind of force field?" said Gabe as he helped Laura back up.

The kids ran their hands over the clear, hard surface. It was smooth and curved toward them.

"It's almost like a fishbowl," said Olive.

"Or like, I don't know, maybe a plasma orb," said Cesar as he pointed to the ceiling, "that belongs to a supervillain . . . like him!"

As the lightning continued to sizzle around the room, a new face appeared in the darkness. It was Dr. von Naysayer. But he was no longer human-size.

He had grown fifty feet tall. "My dearest DATA Set," the giant boomed. "Welcome to the revenge of Dr. von Naysayer!"

Chapter 4

Supervillain Scientist

The DATA Set were trapped inside an orb as the giant supervillain scientist lifted them into the air.

"You know I never like to be the I-told-you-so guy," Cesar said to the others. "But I told you so!"

A huge eyeball peered in at the friends.

"Are you really the mighty DATA Set I've heard so much about?" asked Naysayer. "You look . . . small."

"The joke's on you, because we've been even smaller before!" Olive shouted back.

"I don't think that's helping," said Gabe. "We need to focus. Everyone look around for a way out. What do we see?"

The kids looked down through the clear glass. The crowd below them was running out of the convention center.

Gabe touched the glass wall again and instantly a bolt of lightning zapped his hand.

"Look out!" cried Laura, but Gabe waved her off.

"Thanks, but I'm okay," he said. "I think the rules of the plasma ball are at work here."

"Please explain *that* to those of us who are scared out of their minds right now," said Cesar.

Gabe smiled. "The plasma ball was invented by Nikola Tesla. It works by allowing electricity to flow inside it, so when a person touches the ball from the outside, the electric lights get brighter. The electricity is attracted to the human touch!"

Laura, Olive, and Cesar all looked at one another and then stared back at Gabe blankly.

"It means the electricity is out there, and we are safe in here," Gabe explained.

"I don't *feel* safe in here," said Laura. "I feel *trapped*. And I don't like being trapped."

"I agree," said Olive. "It's time to crack open this glass egg."

Olive leaped into the air and stomped on the bottom of the orb as hard as she could. *SLAM!* But nothing happened.

A low chuckle echoed around the convention center and made the glass orb shake.

"Silly DATA Set," said Naysayer. "There is no escape. But you are not the ones I am after. You are silly little worms dancing on the end of my fishhook. Dance, little worms. Dance!"

Cesar started shaking his booty and making drumbeat noises with his mouth, but Gabe stopped him.

"What are you doing?" Gabe asked.

"Duh, I'm dancing," said Cesar. "And I need a beat to dance to. If it helps us get out of here, I'll do anything. Even bad dance moves that make me look totally silly. Now, if you'll excuse me, I need to get down so we can *get down!*"

"That's not what he meant, Cesar," said Laura. "He's after Dr. Bunsen! And he's using us as bait."

Chapter 5

That's a Big Tomato

The giant scientist held the orb high in the sky as bolts of electricity shocked through the convention center.

"Do you think Bunsen even knows what's going on?" asked Olive. "He can be a little clueless sometimes."

Gabe shook his head. "A building-size version of his ex-partner holding a plasma orb that shoots lightning in a room full of scientists? That would be hard to miss, even for a person as spacey as Dr. B."

"Hello! Did someone say spacey?" a voice called out from below.

It was Dr. Bunsen! He waved happily to the kids.

"Oh, it's you, DATA Set!" he said. "What kind of ride is this? It looks fun! I've been hard at work on my newest invention, so some of us don't have time for silly rides."

"But this ride isn't silly at all," boomed Dr. von Naysayer's deep voice. "It's actually pretty . . . shocking!"

With a flick of his wrist, Naysayer launched lightning down toward Dr. Bunsen. The explosion missed, but sent Bunsen crashing into a display about growing natural fruits and vegetables with a special garden laser.

Luckily, the display was filled with tomatoes, which helped give Bunsen a squishy landing.

"Ah, Naysayer," said Bunsen. "I thought I might see you here. Why don't you let my friends go and we can . . . ketchup?"

Now it was Bunsen's turn. Using the garden laser from the display, he grew the tomatoes monstrously big.

Then Bunsen kicked them at
Naysayer. The juicy fruits exploded
in the giant's face.

"Oh, gross! I hate tomatoes!"
Naysayer cried as he dropped the
orb with the DATA Set still inside.

"Hold on!" screamed Laura as
they fell through the air.

Bunsen quickly used the invention again. This time he grew a banana that became a ramp for the orb. It rolled safely to the floor.

But the DATA Set weren't out of danger yet. Dr. von Naysayer's giant foot landed with a thump next to them.

"We're gonna get squashed!" Olive gulped.

"No, we won't," said Gabe as he pushed on the side of the orb. "It's time to roll!"

The orb skidded away from the giant scientist as the DATA Set headed for the exit.

"Don't leave yet," said Naysayer as he wiped away the tomato mess. "You'll miss all the fun! Perhaps an army of robot dogs will make for a great game of fetch."

Naysayer pulled out a remote control and pressed a button. First, mechanical barking noises rang out. Then the sound of metal paws scraped across the floor as four robot dogs scrambled to block the only way out.

Chapter 6

Bad Robot Dogs! Bad!

"This is my worst nightmare!" Cesar screamed.

The four robot dogs raced after the rolling orb.

"Less yelling, more running!" cried Gabe.

Laura kept her eyes on the path and told the others where to go.

"Turn here!" she called out.

The friends all leaned to one side, and the orb moved in that direction.

Unfortunately, the robot dogs knew how to turn too.

One of the robot dogs stretched its neck and snapped at the ball. Its metal teeth clanked together.

"That was close!" said Olive. "I'm not sure we can out-roll these pups!"

"She's right," Laura agreed. "Dogs always catch the ball . . . unless the ball breaks!"

Gabe, Cesar, and Olive looked at Laura. "WHAT?!" they shouted.

"Just trust me, I have an idea," said Laura. "Turn left now!"

The DATA Set pushed the orb in another direction. The move surprised the robot dogs, who bumped into one another.

Laura pulled out a marker and began drawing circles on the orb as they rolled.

"What are you doing?" asked Gabe.

"Making a target," said Laura.

"Are you trying to make it easier for the robot dogs to aim at us?" asked Cesar.

"Nope, I'm making a bull's-eye for the robot darts display we're about to roll past," Laura explained. "Now, duck!"

A whistling sound rang out as the robot darts flew and struck the target on the orb's wall. The thick glass cracked, then shattered, sending the DATA Set tumbling safely forward.

"See, it worked!" said Laura. "There's no more ball for the robot dogs to chase!"

"But there's also no more orb protecting us from the robot dogs," said Olive.

"Oh, yeah," Laura said as she scratched her head. "I didn't think about that."

The friends watched as the robot
dogs crept closer. They moved so
quietly. It was like someone had
turned off the sound in the room.

Then there was a very loud
growl. But it didn't come from the
robot dogs. It was Cesar's stomach.
Everyone looked at him.

Cesar gave a shrug. "What? I get hungry when I'm nervous."

"Here, try this," said Olive as she tossed him a granola bar. "I was saving it for an emergency. But I didn't think it would involve angry robot dogs."

Cesar caught the granola bar, opened it, and was about to take a bite when something strange happened.

The robot dogs were watching
the granola bar closely with their
robot tongues hanging out.

Cesar waved the granola bar in the air, and each robot dog kept their eyes on it.

"Sit," commanded Cesar . . . and the robot dogs sat!

"Roll over," Cesar said . . . and the robot dogs rolled over!

Then Cesar smiled and said, "Power down."

And the robot dogs obeyed.

Chapter 7

Tiny Car Problems

Gabe, Olive, and Laura gave Cesar a big hug.

"You did it!" said Laura.

"I will never make fun of granola bars again!" said Olive.

"I know, right?" Cesar said as he took a bite of his snack.

Dr. Bunsen ran over and waved.

"Friends, this is no time for playing with puppies!" he cried. "I have a plan to stop Naysayer, but we need to go back to my lab!"

The kids followed Dr. Bunsen out into the parking lot.

"My car is right over here!" he said.

Dr. Bunsen held a set of keys in the air and pressed a button. The lights on a very, very tiny car lit up with a *BEEP-BEEP*.

"Uhh, you expect all of us to fit in that?" Cesar asked.

Olive opened the back door and said, "Maybe it's bigger on the inside."

It wasn't.

The kids squeezed into the back seat and buckled their seatbelts.

"Now I know how canned fish feel!" Laura yelped.

"This is no time for naysaying!" Dr. Bunsen cried. "We have inventions to fix!"

The car pulled out of the parking lot just as Dr. von Naysayer crashed through the roof of the building.

"You cannot escape in a toy car, Bunsen," the giant said as he chased after them.

The kids turned around to watch

Naysayer's shoes crush the road behind them.

"I hope you've got a good plan, Dr. Bunsen," said Gabe.

"It's the perfect plan!" said the doctor. "I invented a machine for the Invention Convention that can bring dreams to life!"

"That sounds amazing, but how will it stop Naysayer?" asked Olive.

"The dream machine makes people feel like they are in a dream, even while they are awake," Dr. Bunsen explained. "All I need are special batteries from my lab. Then we can turn the machine on and send Naysayer into his sweetest dream. And no one can be mad in their sweetest dream."

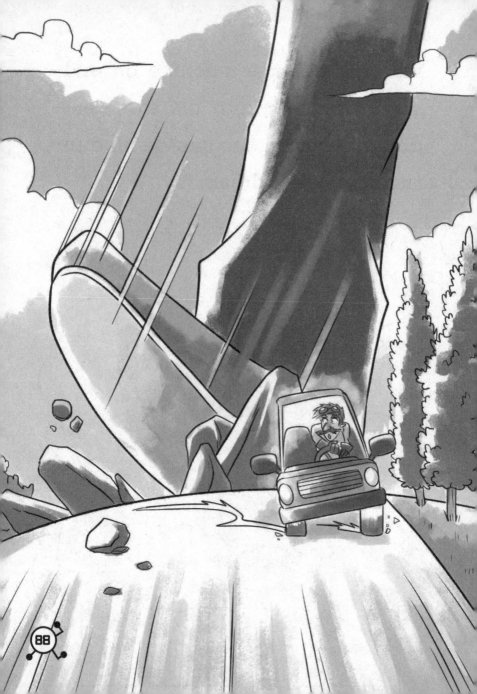

"Unless their dream is to have revenge on their ex-lab partner," Gabe pointed out.

"Oh my, you're right," said Dr. Bunsen. "Hmm, maybe if I adjust the settings to a kind and calm dream . . ."

BOOM!

Another footstep crashed closer to the tiny car. The DATA Set looked at one another and hoped that Dr. Bunsen's plan would work . . . or else this day was going to turn into a nightmare.

Chapter 8

Bunsen's Secret Lab

The group arrived at Dr. Bunsen's old mansion and ran to the secret lab in the basement.

"Just let me find the batteries and then we'll head back," said Dr. Bunsen.

Cesar gulped. "We have to go back?!"

"Of course," said Dr. Bunsen. "The dream machine is the big invention I was going to present, but the batteries ran out of energy. Sadly, the dream machine needs a lot of power."

"But Dr. von Naysayer is right outside!" said Laura.

The friends huddled together, waiting for the roof to be ripped off.

Instead there was a knock at the lab door.

"I'll get it," said Dr. Bunsen.

"Wait!" the kids yelled, but it was too late.

A regular-size version of Dr. von Naysayer stepped inside.

"So, this is your new secret lab?" Naysayer said as he looked around. "How can you work in all this mess?"

"This isn't a mess," said Gabe. "It's a . . . um . . . a collection of great inventions."

"Yeah," Laura agreed. "Like this one. This is an alien communicator. We used it to invite aliens to Earth and even help them get home!"

"And this one," said Olive as she held up another invention.

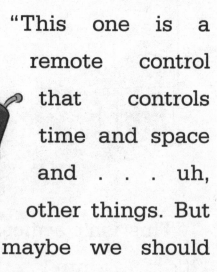

"This one is a remote control that controls time and space and . . . uh, other things. But maybe we should leave that one alone. We kind of almost destroyed the world with it."

Suddenly, a soft smile spread over Dr. von Naysayer's face.

"I know these inventions," he said. "The Growth Ray, the Extra-Outer-Space Radio, even the Time Travel Portal . . . and the Shrink Ray . . . and the Bug Away Machine! Gustav, did you get all of these to work?"

"Well, yeah," Dr. Bunsen said. "I told you it was possible."

Dr. von Naysayer was still studying the inventions intently. "These were things we talked about. And now . . . ," he trailed off, deep in thought.

Laura stepped between the two scientists.

"Dr. von Naysayer," she started, "I know Dr. Bunsen's ideas can seem . . . strange. But that's how creative minds work."

Dr. von Naysayer shuffled back to Dr. Bunsen.

"That is true. I suppose I was a bit jealous of your creativity. So I told myself that surely they would never work. But then you refused to work with me because I was such a . . . Naysayer. I see this now, and I am sorry."

"So, does this mean you're not going to destroy us?" Gabe asked.

Dr. von Naysayer looked surprised. "What in the world are you talking about? I would never wish anyone harm."

"But you turned yourself into a giant!" said Olive.

101

"And sent robot dogs after us!" said Laura.

"And you made me dance!" said Cesar. "And I am not a good dancer."

"And it all started when you trapped us in your plasma orb!" said Gabe.

Dr. von Naysayer reached into his lab coat and pulled out another glowing round orb.

"You mean this plasma orb?" he asked. "My friends, this is only a battery."

Chapter 9

Dream a Not So Little Dream

"Oh dear," said Dr. Bunsen. "This may be my fault."

The DATA Set were very confused. Dr. von Naysayer was also very confused.

But one thing was true: When weird things happened, it was Bunsen's fault most of the time.

"How could you have grown me into a giant who wanted revenge?" asked Dr. von Naysayer. "I don't recall any of this."

Dr. Bunsen searched through a stack of papers on the desk next to him. Then he pulled one out and showed it to the others.

On the paper was a drawing of a machine.

"This is my dream machine," Bunsen explained. "It was made for only one dreamer at a time. To make a dream for more than one person would take a very powerful battery."

Gabe suddenly nodded his head and said, "Like a plasma orb battery, right?"

"So when Dr. von Naysayer turned on his plasma battery, it super-charged Dr. Bunsen's dream machine," Laura explained.

"And then our worries turned the dream into one gigantic nightmare," said Gabe.

"Yes and no," said Dr. Bunsen. "I set the machine to focus on Cesar. So the dreams were made by him."

"Me?" asked Cesar. "Why me?"

"Because I was sure you would have a very safe dream about food," said Dr. Bunsen.

"But then what are you doing at Dr. Bunsen's house, Dr. von Naysayer?" Olive asked.

"I was worried about you," said Dr. von Naysayer. "And we were never at Dr. Bunsen's house. We never even left the stage."

"Oh no," said Cesar. "Was I dancing in front of the smartest scientists in the world?"

"If you call it dancing, then yes," said Naysayer. "Here, let me show you."

Dr. von Naysayer twisted the top of the plasma battery and the DATA Set were suddenly back on stage at the Invention Convention.

"Fiddlesticks," said Dr. Bunsen. "Now the world will never understand my dream machine invention!"

Dr. von Naysayer smiled and held up the glowing plasma battery. "Perhaps I can help with that."

Chapter 10

Keep Dreaming

An oboe solo echoed throughout the convention center. Strains from a cello were layered on top. The musical duet drifted fluidly from note to note as more instruments joined in—violins, French horns, timpani—until the hall filled with an orchestral crescendo.

And then, suddenly, it all faded away, replaced by a saxophone playing smooth jazz.

"It's so beautiful." A spectator wiped a tear from her eye.

Another person started to cry. "Simply inspired."

Everyone at the convention was thrilled by Dr. Bunsen's

dream machine, which was now successfully powered by Dr. von Naysayer's plasma battery. And none other than Naysayer himself was connected to the machine, his dreams projecting music unlike anything the crowd had ever heard.

The presentation ended, and Dr. Bunsen and Dr. von Naysayer bowed side by side as the audience burst into wild applause.

Cheering loudest of all was the DATA Set.

"See, they make beautiful music when they work together," Olive said to her friends.

Just then, the convention director came out holding a trophy.

"We proudly present this award to Dr. Gustav Bunsen and Dr. Hans von Naysayer for best teamwork," she announced.

The two scientists accepted the award, and the DATA Set raced to the stage to congratulate them.

"You really do make a great team!" Gabe exclaimed.

"Oh, it is exciting to win an award together after all these years," Dr. Bunsen admitted.

"I could not agree more." Dr. von Naysayer nodded. "And I will be honored to display this trophy on the highest shelf in my laboratory."

"*Your* laboratory?" Dr. Bunsen raised an eyebrow. "You must be confused. I already have the perfect spot picked out for this award in *my* laboratory."

Dr. von Naysayer shook his head. "Now, now, Gustav. We can both agree that your dream machine needed my plasma battery to work.

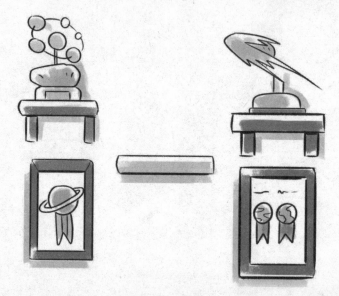

Therefore, it is I who should keep the trophy."

Dr. Bunsen cleared his throat. "Well, my name is clearly above yours, which means that I am the most brilliant winner."

"Now see here, Gustav," Dr. von Naysayer began.

"Relax!" Laura interrupted. "Why don't you both take turns displaying the trophy?"

Dr. Bunsen and Dr. von Naysayer stared at each other.

"I suppose that could work," Dr. Bunsen said.

"Yes, I suppose," said Dr. von Naysayer.

The DATA Set shook their heads. They had no idea that getting two genius scientists to agree would be so hard.

"At least they're not enemies anymore." Gabe shrugged. "And who knows? Maybe they'll work together again one day!"

Cesar let out a little chuckle and said, "Keep dreaming."